Karen's Wish

**Here are some other books
about Karen
that you might enjoy:**

Karen's Witch

Karen's Roller Skates

Karen's Worst Day

Karen's Kittycat Club

Karen's School Picture

Karen's Little Sister

Karen's Birthday

Karen's Haircut

Karen's Sleepover

Karen's Grandmothers

Karen's Prize

Karen's Ghost

Karen's Surprise

Karen's New Year

Little Sister

Karen's Wish
Ann M. Martin

Illustrations by Susan Tang

A
LITTLE APPLE
PAPERBACK

SCHOLASTIC INC.
New York Toronto London Auckland Sydney

Activities by Nancy E. Krulik

ISBN 0-590-43647-3

12 11 10 9 8 7 6 5 4 3 2 1   0 1 2 3 4 5/9

Printed in the U.S.A.   40

First Scholastic printing, December 1990

This book is for
Eve, Bill, and Margot,
who know why.

Christmas Is Coming

"Look! Look at that!" cried Andrew. "That is what I want for Christmas!"

Andrew is my little brother. He isn't even five yet. I am Karen Brewer and I am seven years old. I have freckles and wear glasses. My hair is blonde and my eyes are blue. Christmas is my favorite time of year.

Andrew was pointing to something on TV. It was a commercial for Dyno-cars. Dyno-cars are little racing cars that explode when they run into a wall or something.

Then you put them back together so you can explode them again.

"Remember to put Dyno-cars on your list for Santa," I told Andrew.

"I will," he replied.

Andrew and I were at home. It was a school-day afternoon. In fact, it was almost suppertime. We were coloring pictures about Christmas. I was coloring a tree with presents under it. Andrew was trying to make a Santa.

"*Christmas is coming,*" I sang as I worked, "*the geese are getting fat; Please to put a penny in the old man's hat; If you haven't a penny, a ha'penny will do; If you haven't got a ha'penny, God bless you.*"

"You know what?" said Andrew, looking up from his picture.

"What?" I asked.

"I don't understand that song. What is a ha'penny?"

"I'm not sure," I replied.

"Let's sing a song we both know," said Andrew.

So we sang "Jingle Bells." First we sang it the regular way. Then we sang, "*Jingle bells, Batman smells, Robin laid an egg. Batmobile lost a wheel, and Commissioner broke his leg.*"

We giggled. But I stopped suddenly. Another commercial had come on TV. "There! That's what *I* want!" I exclaimed. "Baby Grow-a-Tooth!"

The next commercial was for an art kit. With the kit you could decorate hats and

3

make badges. Both Andrew and I cried, "I want *that!*"

Then I said, "Boy, it sure is hard waiting for Christmas."

"I know," Andrew answered. "How many days, Karen?"

"A lot," I told him. "It isn't even December yet. It won't be December until the day after tomorrow."

"Boo," said Andrew.

"But think of all the things we can do before Christmas. We can buy a tree, we can make decorations, we can make presents to give to people, we can make Christmas cards — "

"And Christmas cookies," interrupted Andrew. He paused. "Where are we going to be on Christmas Day this year?" he asked.

"Here. At Mommy's house. Remember?" I replied. "We go to Daddy's on the day before Christmas. We spend the night there. Then we come back here on Christmas morning. We will have two Christmases."

"I'm glad they will be on different days,"

said Andrew. "I did not like having two Thanksgivings in one day."

"Me, neither," I said. "That was awful. I will never eat turkey again." Just thinking about turkey made my stomach feel funny. (A week ago, Andrew and I had eaten a Thanksgiving dinner at Mommy's house, and another at Daddy's house. All in one day. I ate so much I got a gigundo stomachache. Mommy and Daddy said we would never have two celebrations in one day again. I was glad they decided that.)

Why did we have two Thanksgivings? Why were we going to have two Christmases? Because Andrew and I are two-twos, that's why.

Christmas Here, Christmas There

Since not everyone knows what a two-two is, I will explain how Andrew and I became Andrew Two-Two and Karen Two-Two. It's because of our parents. Our mommy and daddy used to be married. But then they decided that they did not love each other anymore. So they got divorced. Daddy stayed in the big house we used to live in. Mommy moved to a little house. Andrew and I went with her. The big house and the little house are both in Stoneybrook, Connecticut.

Then Daddy got married again. He married Elizabeth. Elizabeth is our stepmother. Mommy got married again, too. She married Seth. Seth is our stepfather. Now Andrew and I live with Mommy and Seth at the little house most of the time. We live there with Rocky and Midgie, Seth's cat and dog, and with Emily Junior, my rat.

But every other weekend, Andrew and I live with Daddy and our other family. Our other family is big, so it is a good thing Daddy's house is big, too. Here's who lives at the big house: Daddy, Elizabeth, and Elizabeth's four children. Her children are David Michael, who is seven like me; Kristy, who is thirteen; and Charlie and Sam, who are *old*. They are seventeen and fifteen. Charlie, Sam, and David Michael are my stepbrothers. Kristy is my stepsister, and I love her so, so much! She is like a regular sister. Sometimes she baby-sits for me. She is fun.

There are even more people at the big house. There is Emily Michelle. She is my

7

adopted sister. Daddy and Elizabeth adopted her. Emily came all the way from a country called Vietnam. She is two and a half. I named my rat after her. Nannie also lives at the big house. She is Elizabeth's mother. That means she is my stepgrandmother. I love Nannie very much, too. She helps take care of the big house, and she watches Emily while Daddy and Elizabeth are at work. Oh, there are also two pets at the big house. Boo-Boo is Daddy's old, fat cat, and Shannon is David Michael's puppy.

See why Andrew and I are two-twos? Because we have two of so many things. (I got the name from a book that my teacher, Ms. Colman, read to my second-grade class at Stoneybrook Academy. It was called *Jacob Two-Two Meets the Hooded Fang*.) Andrew and I have two mommies and two daddies, two houses and two families, two cats and two dogs. We each have two bicycles (actually Andrew has two tricycles), one at the big house, one at the little house. I have two stuffed cats, one at each house (Moosie at the big house, Goosie at the little house). We have toys and clothes and books at each house. That is so we don't have to pack very much when we go back and forth between the houses. Guess what. I even have two best friends. Nancy Dawes lives next door to Mommy. Hannie Papadakis lives across the street and one house down from Daddy. (Nancy and Hannie and I are all in Ms. Colman's class. We call ourselves the Three Musketeers.)

It is fun being Karen Two-Two — most of the time. I like having two families. I especially like going to the big house. It is an exciting place. It is usually busy and noisy. But the little house is good for peace and quiet. (Andrew likes peace and quiet more than I do.) It is also nice to have two bicycles and two bedrooms and two birthday parties each year. And in a few weeks, Andrew and I would have two Christmases.

But, sometimes I do not like being Karen Two-Two. Two Thanksgiving dinners in one day was no fun at all. Plus, I did not have

two of my special blanket, Tickly. I tried
bringing Tickly back and forth between my
houses, but sometimes I left him behind.
Finally, I had to rip Tickly in half, so I could
have a piece at each house. I did not like
ripping Tickly apart.

Still, I feel pretty lucky.

I went back to my coloring. *"Christmas is
coming,"* I sang.

3

Christmas and Hanukkah

"Jump! Jump!" I cried. "No, jump *up* — "

"Game over!" Nancy announced.

I was at the Daweses' house. Nancy and I were playing Nintendo.

"Boo," I said. I had just lost another game. I am not as good a player as Nancy is. Maybe that's because I do not have Nintendo. But Nancy gets to practice whenever she wants.

"You know what?" I said. "Maybe I will ask for Nintendo for Christmas."

"I just want some more games for Nin-

11

tendo," said Nancy. "There are three that I want."

"It's too bad you don't celebrate Christmas," I told Nancy. "If you did, you could get your games in just a few weeks. Now you have to wait all the way until your birthday to get presents." I felt sort of sad.

But Nancy said, "I don't have to wait until my birthday. We get presents at Hanukkah."

"You do?" I replied. I did not know that. I knew that Nancy is Jewish. And I knew she celebrates Hanukkah. I just did not know *how* she celebrates Hanukkah. I guess that is because Nancy and I were not such good friends last year. Last year Nancy was in first grade. But I started out in kindergarten and *skipped* into first grade. And I was not even in Nancy's room. We got to be best friends in Ms. Colman's class this year.

"Sure," said Nancy. "I'll get presents. And I'll get them before you do. Hanukkah comes before Christmas. I can't wait!"

I smiled at Nancy. But I still felt sad. I was pretty sure Nancy wouldn't get as many presents at Hanukkah as I would get on Christmas Day. Nancy would not have a tree with presents *piled* under it. And she would not have a stocking filled with presents, either.

"I wish we celebrated the same holiday," said Nancy. "I wish you celebrated Hanukkah. It would be fun if we both celebrated the same holiday."

"Yeah," I agreed. But I wished that *Nancy* celebrated *Christmas*, not the other way around. I could not imagine *not* celebrating Christmas. What would December be without tinsel and wreaths and decorated trees and holly and Santa Claus and cookies baking . . . and, of course, presents?

"You know what else I want?" asked Nancy.

"What?" I replied.

"Baby Grow-a-Tooth."

"Really? I want Baby Grow-a-Tooth, too! She is gigundo cool. If you press her arms together, her front teeth grow in."

"Yeah. And she comes with her very own teething ring," added Nancy.

"I know. Plus, Andrew and I both want this special art kit. And I want a new horn for my bicycle, and *lots* of books. I want more books about Paddington Bear and more books about Doctor Dolittle. Oh, and I want *The Polar Express*, and of course I want more *Bobbsey Twins*. (Nancy and I love

the *Bobbsey Twins*. We both have almost every *Bobbsey Twins* book there is.)

"I want more *Bobbsey Twins* books, too," said Nancy, "plus *The Land of Oz* and the book about witches by Roald Dahl. Oh, and a Spirograph."

Gosh, I hoped Nancy would get everything she wanted. But I wasn't sure she would. I wasn't sure I would, either, but I thought I had a better chance than she did. To be on the safe side, I decided to start writing my Christmas list as soon as I got home that afternoon.

Nannie's Fall

Nancy and I were in the middle of an exciting game of Nintendo when I looked at my watch. "Uh-oh!" I cried.

"What is it?" asked Nancy.

"I have to go home," I told her. "It's after five o'clock."

"Boo," said Nancy.

"Double boo," I replied.

"Come over again tomorrow afternoon, okay?"

"Okay!" I called as I ran down the hallway.

I rushed out of Nancy's house, across her lawn and my lawn, and into the little house.

"Mommy!" I shouted. "I'm sorry I'm late. Nancy and I were — "

Mommy waved at me impatiently. She was talking on the phone. And she was frowning. Was she mad because I had been too noisy?

"I'm sorry I didn't use my indoor voice," I whispered.

But Mommy just waved at me again. "Mm-hmm . . . mm-hmm," she was saying. "Yes, I understand. Okay. Hold on. I'll put Karen on."

Who could Mommy be talking to? I wondered.

Mommy held the phone out to me. "It's Daddy," she said.

"Oh, goody!" I replied. Then I spoke into the phone. "Hello? Daddy?"

"Hi, sweetie," said my father. "Listen, I'm afraid I have some bad news."

Uh-oh, I thought. "What is it?" I asked.

"Nannie had a fall this afternoon. She

broke her hip. Luckily Kristy and Charlie were home, so they called an ambulance. Nannie is in the hospital. I'm visiting her now. She will be there for several weeks. I thought you should know."

"Oh, *Daddy!*" I exclaimed. I began to cry.

Nothing Daddy said made me feel any better. Finally, he asked to talk to Andrew. He wanted to tell him the news, too.

That evening I could not eat supper. I could not do my homework. All I could think about was Nannie. Mommy came into my room. She found me sitting on my bed, staring into space.

"Why don't you call Kristy?" Mommy suggested. "Maybe you will feel better if you talk to her."

I sighed. "Okay," I said. So I called Kristy at the big house.

"When will Nannie come home?" I asked her.

"I don't know for sure," Kristy answered.

"The doctors said in a few weeks. I guess that means about three weeks. Nannie broke her hip pretty badly. She might have to have an operation. The doctors might want to put a pin in her hip to help hold the bones together."

"Oh," I said. An *operation*. I felt worse than ever. "Can I visit Nannie?"

"I don't think so," Kristy replied. "I know you visited Emily Michelle when she was in the hospital. But Nannie is in a special part of the hospital. Kids are not allowed to visit there."

When Kristy and I hung up, I went back to my room. I tried to feel better. I told myself that hospitals make sick or hurt people well. So the hospital was the best place for Nannie. When I broke my wrist, *I* went to the hospital, and now my wrist is all better.

But then I remembered something awful. I remembered Kristy's friend Claudia. Claudia used to have a grandmother. But her grandmother got really sick, so she went to the hospital. Only she *never came back*. She *died* there.

Please don't die, Nannie, I thought. Please come home.

5

Karen's Wish

One night, Mommy said to Andrew and me, "How about writing your Christmas lists this evening?"

It was cozy in our house. Outside, snow was falling lightly. The wind was blowing. Seth had built a fire in the fireplace. I was feeling Christmasy.

"Christmas lists?" repeated Andrew. "For Santa Claus? Can we send them up the chimney?"

"Of course," said Mommy.

A long time ago, Mommy showed Andrew and me a special way to send letters to Santa. You do not put the letters in envelopes and write SANTA CLAUS, THE NORTH POLE on them. You do not stick stamps on the envelopes and drop the letters in a mailbox.

You do something *magic*.

This is what Mommy said to do. First we write our letters to Santa. Then we make sure we have a nice fire burning in the fireplace. Then we give the letters to Mommy and Seth. They stick the letters over the flames in the fireplace, and *whoosh!* The letters rush up the chimney and sail through the night sky to the North Pole. They probably land right in Santa's workshop. (Andrew thinks they land on Santa's *desk*.)

"Karen, help me write my letter," said Andrew. "Please?"

"Okay," I agreed. "And then I will write mine."

"Seth, will you keep the fire going?" asked Andrew. "We need that fire."

Seth smiled. "Don't worry. It's a special Santa Claus fire."

"Goody," said Andrew.

Mommy gave me some papers and a pencil. Andrew and I sat at the kitchen table. "Okay, I'm ready," I told Andrew.

"All right. Make the letter say," my brother said, " 'Dear Santa, How are you? Fine, I hope. How is Mrs. Claus? How are your reindeer, especially Rudolph? How are the elves?' "

"Slow down!" I cried.

So Andrew did. Then he began a list of all the toys he wanted. The list was very long. When I finished Andrew's letter, I wrote my own. This was my letter:

DEAR SANTA,
MERRY CHRISTMAS! HERE IS WHAT I WOULD LIKE THIS YEAR. I WISH FOR NANNIE TO GET WELL AND COME HOME FROM THE HOSPITAL BEFORE CHRISTMAS. THANK YOU VERY MUCH. LOVE,
                              Karen Brewer

"We're ready!" Andrew and I called, as soon as I finished my letter. We ran into the living room. Mommy read our letters. She frowned a little, but then she and Seth stuck the letters over the fire. The letters disappeared up the chimney.

"I want to see them fly into the sky!" cried Andrew.

But Mommy said, "Honey, it's too dark outside. Anyway, I want to talk to you and Karen. Sit on the couch with me."

Andrew and I sat down on either side of Mommy. (We made a Mommy sandwich.) Were we in trouble? I wondered.

"You know," said Mommy, "Santa can't grant every wish. You might not get everything you ask for."

"That," I replied, "is why I only asked for one thing."

I was afraid to ask for anything else. I was sure that if I did, I would jinx my one true wish.

Nannie's Call

On Friday afternoon, Mommy drove Andrew and me to Daddy's. It was a big-house weekend. Usually, I love weekends at Daddy's. But I knew this one would be different. And it was.

When Andrew and I opened the door to the big house, we found everyone waiting for us. There were Daddy, Elizabeth, Kristy, Charlie, Sam, David Michael, Emily, and even Shannon and Boo-Boo.

But Nannie was not there. I missed her right away.

At dinner that night I did not talk very much.

"What's the matter?" asked Sam. "Cat got your tongue?"

I shook my head. But Andrew giggled. "Boo-Boo's way over there!" he said, pointing.

Everyone laughed.

After dinner, I wandered into the den. Sometimes Nannie and I would sit there together. I would read to her, or I would watch her knit. But Nannie was in the hospital. I turned on the TV. Then I turned it off. I picked up a magazine. I put it down.

"Want to play a game?" David Michael asked me.

"No, thanks," I said.

"Want me to read to you?" asked Kristy.

"No. . . . Thank you."

Finally I just went to bed.

The next day, I did not feel any better. In the afternoon, Daddy and Elizabeth went to visit Nannie. Charlie and Sam went to a friend's house. Kristy was left baby-sitting for Andrew, Emily, David Michael, and me.

"Let's make Christmas tree ornaments!" she said.

"Yeah!" cried Andrew and David Michael.

Kristy covered the kitchen table with newspaper. She set out glue and scissors and construction paper and yarn and glitter and Styrofoam balls and bits of ribbon and felt and other things, too.

At first, I did not want to make an ornament, but Kristy said. "Let's make new ornaments to surprise Nannie when she comes home."

So we did. David Michael made a chain out of green and red and white construction paper.

Andrew cut out a star and covered both sides with glitter. "For the top of the tree," he said.

I took ribbon and wound it around a ball. I glued on felt polka dots. Then I sprinkled glitter over it.

"Beautiful," said Kristy. She had cut a

section out of an egg carton. She was making a bell.

Emily just made a mess.

Kristy was trying to wash glue out of Emily's hair when the phone rang.

"I'll get it!" I cried. And guess who it was. Nannie! She was calling from the hospital. Daddy and Elizabeth had just left.

"Are you really coming home soon?" I asked Nannie.

"I really am."

"When?"

"The week before Christmas," Nannie replied.

"You're sure?"

"Positive."

David Michael tugged on my arm. "Let *me* talk to her," he said.

"Nannie? David Michael wants to talk to you."

"Okay. I'll see you soon," said Nannie.

Soon, I repeated to myself. Nannie would be home soon. She had said so. I wanted to believe her . . . but I was afraid to.

7

Eight Nights

Ms. Colman is the best teacher ever. Really. Today she made one of her Surprising Announcements.

My class had just come in from recess. We were unpeeling our mittens and scarves and hats and jackets. We were about to sit down at our desks when we noticed something. On our desks were construction paper and glue and scissors and cotton balls and some other stuff.

"What's this for?" asked Ricky Torres.

Ms. Colman would not answer until we

were sitting down and were quiet. Then she said, "Class, I have an announcement to make." (Yea! I thought.) "This afternoon, you may make decorations for Christmas and Hanukkah. We will put them in our windows where everyone can see them. You may make whatever you want — bells, menorahs, trees, Stars of David, dreidels, Santas, anything. You may also sit wherever you want."

Oh, boy! Of course I ran to the back of the room to be with Hannie and Nancy. (I used to sit with them, but Ms. Colman moved me to the front row when I got my glasses.)

"Come on, you guys. Let's get to work!" I said.

We began drawing shapes and snipping them out. I worked on a Christmas tree, Nancy worked on a star with six points, and Hannie worked on a present. She made a bow for it out of yarn.

"That's pretty," I said to Hannie. I was thinking about how our living room would look in a few weeks. A decorated tree would stand in front of the window, and under it would be presents. I was sure there would be presents for me, even if I did not ask for any.

"Thank you," said Hannie. "You know what I want for Christmas? I want clothes for my Barbie and a box of paints and a new dress and a set of magic tricks and a rabbit and . . . " Hannie's list was long.

Then Nancy said, "For Hanukkah, I'm asking for three Nintendo games and Baby Grow-a-Tooth and a Spirograph and a lot of books, *plus* this really cool skirt I saw, and poodle barrettes. Oh, and Barbie clothes."

"Are you *really* going to get all that stuff?" I asked Nancy doubtfully.

"Maybe. We get presents on eight nights."

"Eight nights!" I cried.

"Yup," said Nancy. "That's how long Hanukkah lasts. Different families give out presents in different ways. But at my house, we get one present on each of the first seven nights. Then on the eighth night, we get lots of presents.''

"Boy," I said. (I was impressed.) Then I asked, "How come you celebrate Hanukkah for eight nights?''

"Well, it all started with Antiochus," replied Nancy. "He was a mean king who lived years and years ago. He wanted all of his people to follow his religion. But the Jewish people didn't want to do that. So they decided to fight back. Their leader was

from this family named the Maccabees. They fought hard for several years and finally they won! There was peace in their land. But — the soldiers had taken over the Jews' Temple of Jerusalem, and the Maccabees wanted it back. To do that they would need oil to light the menorah, which was a special lamp. All they could find was a *tiny* bit of oil, but it lasted for *eight nights*. That's why Hanukkah lasts for eight nights and is called the Festival of Lights."

I was listening to Nancy while she talked. I really was. But I was also getting a good idea. . . .

8

A Present for Nancy

This was my good idea: I would buy Nancy a present. Hannie and I always exchange Christmas presents. This is because we are best friends. Nancy and I are best friends, too. But I could not get Nancy a Christmas present. I could get her a present, though. The question was, what should I get her?

When I came home from school that day, I went to my room to think. I wanted to get Nancy the perfect present. What could I buy her? I knew what to get Hannie. That was because Hannie had told me what she wanted: ponytail holders. I tried to remember what Nancy had said she wanted for Hanukkah. Almost everything was too expensive. (I do not have much money.)

I thought about poodle barrettes and Barbie clothes. I could afford things like that, but they did not seem very special. Besides, Nancy had probably told her parents that she wanted poodle barrettes and Barbie clothes.

I shut my eyes. Knee socks? Nah, not special enough. Baby Grow-a-Tooth? Nah, *way* too expensive.

I was not getting anywhere, so I opened my eyes. I gazed around my room. And my eyes landed on my collection of *Bobbsey Twins* books. There they were, all in order on my bookshelf, according to number. Oh, except for number 53. Number 53 was missing. I had not been able to find it. Neither had Nancy. Just like me, she had almost every number. But no 53. And we were *dying* to read number 53.

"Wait!" I cried out loud. "That's it!" The perfect present for Nancy was *The Bobbsey Twins #53* — if I could find it. We both wanted that book badly. It was called *The Bobbsey Twins in the Mystery Cave*. I bet if I went to a lot of stores I could find it.

"Mommy! Hey, Mommy!" I yelled. I ran downstairs.

"Indoor voice, Karen," said Mommy.

"Sorry," I replied. I stopped shouting. I said, "Mommy, I want to get a special present for Nancy this year. And I thought and I thought and I decided to buy her *The Bobbsey Twins in the Mystery Cave.* I have enough money for it. Will you help me look for it? That's the book that's hard to find."

"Of course I'll help you look," said Mommy.

"Thank you. Now — do you think it is okay to give Nancy a Hanukkah present, even though I am not Jewish?"

Mommy smiled. "I think so," she said.

9

Hanukkah Shopping

When school was over the next day, Mrs. Dawes drove Nancy and me home.

"Want to play Nintendo?" Nancy asked me as her mother parked the car.

"Yes," I answered, "but I can't. I have something very important to do. I'll see you in school tomorrow, Nancy. 'Bye!"

I ran off before Nancy could ask me what I had to do. See, the important thing was that I was going Hanukkah shopping. Mommy had said she would drive me around looking for *The Bobbsey Twins in the Mystery Cave.* You know what else she said? She said, "If we find a store that carries the book, I will buy a copy for *you*, too."

"Oh, thank you!" I had cried. "That will be great because I only have enough money for one copy."

That afternoon, Mommy dressed Andrew in his snowsuit and boots and hat and mittens and scarf. Andrew could hardly move, but Mommy said, "It's cold and it feels like snow. Everybody bundle up."

So we did. Then Mommy drove to the Book Nook. I ran right to the section where the series books are kept. There were *The Bobbsey Twins*. But no number 53.

Boo.

"Don't worry," said Mommy. "We can still try Peter Rabbit and the Book Barn. We can even look in the grocery store."

"Okay," I said.

But Peter Rabbit was out of number 53. So was the Book Barn.

"That's a popular book in the series," said the saleslady at the Book Barn. She smiled at me.

"I know," I answered. "That's why my friend and I want to read it so badly."

I felt very discouraged when we left the Book Barn.

But Mommy said, "I've got an idea. Let's skip the grocery store. Let's drive to Washington Mall instead. There are two big bookstores at the mall."

"Really, Mommy? You'll really drive all the way to the mall?" I cried.

"Sure," Mommy replied. "Why not? Besides, Andrew needs new shoes."

So we drove to the mall, which is way far away. Mommy parked the car and we walked inside. (Well, Mommy and I walked inside. Andrew just sort of lurched along in his snowsuit.)

We passed the shoe store before we got to the bookstores. Mommy stopped and zipped Andrew out of his suit. She bought him a pair of sneakers. While Andrew was trying the sneakers on, I looked at the decorations in the mall. The mall was very Christmasy. But I did not see any menorahs or dreidels or stars with six points. I wondered why.

"Okay, Karen," said Mommy. "Are you ready to continue your search?"

"Yup," I said. "I'm feeling lucky now."

We walked into Books by the Dozen. (Andrew was wearing his new sneakers and they squeaked.)

"Do you have *The Bobbsey Twins*, number fifty-three?" I asked a store clerk.

"Sorry," she said.

I looked at Mommy. "We've got one last try," she told me.

So we headed for Kidsbooks, Inc. "Have you got *The Bobbsey Twins*, number fifty-three?" I asked the first clerk I saw.

"I think so," he replied. And he led me to *The Bobbsey Twins* books. There was *one* copy of number 53!

"I'll take it!" I said. I did not care that there was only one copy.

"Maybe Nancy will lend me the book when she's finished," I said to Mommy.

Later that afternoon, I wrapped up the book. Then I hid it under my bed.

10

The Perfect Tree

One Friday night, it snowed. Not a lot, but enough to look pretty. When I woke up on Saturday morning, the grass was covered with white, and the trees shook long white fingers at me. I waved back at them.

Snow is like magic.

It was a little-house weekend. Mommy and Seth and Andrew and I ate breakfast together in the warm kitchen.

"Do you know what today is the perfect day for?" asked Seth.

"Snowmen?" said Andrew.

"I was thinking of buying our Christmas tree."

"Oh, yes! YES!" I shouted. "And please, can Nancy come with us?"

Almost before I knew it, Nancy and I and my little-house family were piling into our car.

"I've never looked for a Christmas tree before," said Nancy.

"Well, it is gigundo fun," I told her.

Seth drove us to a tree lot in Stoneybrook. We walked among all the Christmas trees. Our boots crunched through the snow.

"We have to find the perfect tree," I said.

We walked all around saying things like, "Too tall," or, "Too skinny," or, "Too fat." Or, "The needles are too long," or, "Too short," or, "Too pointy."

At last Nancy stood in front of a tree and said, "What about this one?"

Mommy and Seth and Andrew and I looked at the tree. At first we did not say a word. We could not find anything wrong with it.

"Perfect!" I exclaimed finally. "It is the perfect Christmas tree."

So we bought the tree and loaded it into the back of our car. The tree was very long. We drove home with the tailgate open!

At the little house, Seth put the tree in a bucket of water. He left it outside, leaning against our fence.

"Who wants to make Christmas cookies?" asked Mommy.

"I do!" Andrew and Nancy and I cried.

There was cookie dough in the refrigerator. Mommy helped us roll it out flat. Then we used cookie cutters to make bells and trees and snowmen.

While we worked, Andrew said, "I hope Santa knows that Karen and I will be at two houses this year. I sure hope he knows that. I really want those Dyno-cars. And a book about a stegosaurus."

"Is that what Christmas is all about?" asked Nancy. "Santa Claus and presents?" She nibbled on some cookie dough. "And how come you decorate a tree?"

11

More Than Santa Claus

Christmas is about a lot of things, I thought.

"Nancy?" I said. "Remember when you told Hannie and me about Antiochus and the Maccabees and the Temple of Jerusalem?"

"Yes," said Nancy.

"Well, there's a story about Christmas, too."

"Goody," said Nancy. "I like stories."

"Me, too," said Andrew. "Tell the Christmas story, Karen."

"Okay," I replied. "Well, Christmas began a long time ago when two people named Mary and Joseph were traveling to the town of Bethlehem. This was hard for them because Mary was going to have a baby. Only it was going to be a *special* baby. An angel named Gabriel had told her that her baby would be God's son.

"Well," I went on, "after a long time, Mary and Joseph reached Bethlehem, but they couldn't find a place to stay. An innkeeper finally said that they could sleep in his stable, though. So they did. And that night, the baby was born. Mary and Joseph named him Jesus, just like Gabriel had said to. Everyone wanted to see Jesus. Shepherds came and so did three wise men. The Three Wise Men found Jesus by following a bright new star in the sky. That's why we put stars on the tops of our Christmas trees. Or sometimes angels."

"Oh," said Nancy. "I see. But what does Santa Claus have to do with all this?"

Mommy answered that question. "Santa

Claus is the short name for Saint Nicholas. He was a kind bishop who lived a long time ago. Saint Nicholas wanted to tell people about Christ. But not everyone believed in Christ, so Saint Nicholas was put in prison. When he was finally let go, he was even kinder than he had been before, and lots and lots of stories grew up around him. Most of the stories were about Saint Nicholas protecting children. Or about Saint Nicholas secretly bringing gifts to people. Over the years the stories changed. Children in different countries believe different things. But — "

"But we know that Santa lives at the North Pole with Rudolph and the elves," said Andrew. "Right?"

"Right," I replied. "Nancy? Will you tell me more about Hanukkah?"

Dreidels and Menorahs

"Sure," said Nancy. "I'll tell you about dreidels and menorahs. And some other things, too." Nancy placed a row of silver balls down the front of a snowman.

"Perfect timing," said Mommy. "I'll put the cookies in the oven while Nancy tells you about Hanukkah. It will take awhile to bake all these batches of cookies."

"Let's go to my room," I said to Nancy.

"Can I come, too?" asked Andrew.

"Okay," I replied.

Up in my room, I let Emily Junior out of

her cage. Andrew played with her while Nancy said, "I guess the most important thing about Hanukkah is lighting the menorah. When we do that, we remember the menorah in the Temple of Jerusalem. We light one candle on the first night, two candles on the second night, and finally on the eighth night, we light all the candles. We say blessings of thanks to God. And we sing special Hanukkah songs, but we sing them in Hebrew."

"Why?" I asked.

"Because that's the language of the Jewish people. Anyway, after we light the menorah and say the blessings and sing the songs, then we play dreidel games and give each other gifts."

"What are drable games?" Andrew wanted to know.

"Dreidel games," Nancy corrected him. "A dreidel is a kind of top. It has four sides. On each side is a Hebrew letter. Some dreidels are different, but most of them have these letters: *nun*, *gimmel*, *heh*, and

shin. If you put them together, they stand for the words that mean 'a great miracle happened there.' 'There' means at the Temple of Jerusalem. I know lots of dreidel games, but this one is my favorite. Everyone sits on the floor, takes six nuts or raisins, and puts one in a pile in the center. Then you take turns spinning a dreidel. When it stops, you look at the letter that's facing up. If it's *nun*, that means 'nothing,' and the next player takes his or her turn. If it's *gimmel,* that means 'everything' and you get to take all the nuts or raisins in the center. *Heh* means you take half of what's in the pile, and *shin* means you have to *add* to the center pile. You keep playing until one person has all the nuts or raisins. It's really fun.

"Oh, and we eat special food at Hanukkah. My favorite is potato *latkes.* They're like pancakes. And did you know that we send Hanukkah cards, just like you send Christmas cards?"

"No," I replied. "I didn't."

"Karen!" Mommy called then. "Andrew! Nancy! The cookies are done."

"All right!" I called back. "Come on, you guys. Let's go."

Andrew and Nancy and I jumped up, and Andrew put Emily back in her cage. But Nancy said, "Karen, I have to make a phone call."

"Okay," I replied. That was fine with me because I had to ask Mommy something in private. "Meet you downstairs," I said.

When Nancy finally came into the kitchen, we both said, "Guess what!"

We giggled. "You go first," I said.

"All right. I called Mommy and she said you can come over and celebrate the last night of Hanukkah with us."

"Really? I just asked Mommy if you could celebrate Christmas with us and *she* said yes!"

"Neat!" cried Nancy. "We'll trade holidays. Deal?"

"Deal," I said.

13

Countdown to Christmas

Christmas was coming fast. The days were speeding by. I was busy at school. I was busy making presents for people in my families. I was busy making Christmas cards, too. And one evening we brought our tree inside and decorated it.

Finally, there were just ten more days until Christmas. It was Saturday. Early in the afternoon, Mommy found me in my room. I was singing, *"On the tenth day of Christmas my true love sent to me . . . um . . ."*

"Ten lords a-leaping," said Mommy.

I smiled. "Thanks."

"You're welcome. Listen," Mommy went on. "Wouldn't you like to make another Christmas list, Karen? I know there must be some gifts you want."

I thought about that. Nannie was doing well. I had talked to her on the phone lots of times. She had said she would be home from the hospital any day. Maybe I had already gotten my Christmas wish.

"All right," I said to Mommy. "I will make a list for you."

"Come downstairs and keep me company," she replied.

So I did. We sat in the living room together. Mommy read a big person's book. I got a pencil and a piece of paper. Across the top of the paper I wrote

WHAT I WANT FOR CHRISTMAS (PLEASE).

I had just written the letter B for Baby Grow-a-Tooth when the phone rang.

"I'll get it!" I said.

I ran into our kitchen. I picked up the telephone. "Hello?" I said.

"Hi, sweetie. It's Daddy."

"Hi!" I cried.

"Karen," Daddy went on, "I'm afraid I have a little bad news."

Bad news? "It's Nannie, isn't it?" I whispered.

"Yes," replied Daddy. (I could feel a lump in my throat.) "Nannie had a setback."

"A setback?" I repeated. "What do you mean?"

"She developed something called a staph infection. She's just got a sore throat and a little fever, but the doctors want to keep her in the hospital and give her medicine until she's all better."

"Oh," I said. Part of me felt relieved. A staph infection did not sound very bad. Another part of me felt sad. I was pretty sure that my Christmas wish would not come true after all. "Will Nannie be home for Christmas?" I asked.

"I don't know," Daddy answered. "I just

don't know. That will depend on how fast the medicine makes Nannie better."

"Okay," I said.

Daddy asked to talk to Mommy then. So I called her to the phone. Then I went to the living room. I found the Christmas list I had started. I crumpled it up and threw it away.

Even though I felt sad about Nannie, it was hard not to get excited about Christmas. A wreath with a big red bow hung on our

door. Our Christmas tree shone with lights and ornaments. Mommy gathered holly and put it in vases around the house. On TV, Andrew and I watched *Frosty the Snowman* and *How the Grinch Stole Christmas* and *A Charlie Brown Christmas*.

I decided to count down the days until Christmas. I made a very, very short calendar. (It had only nine squares.) Starting the next day, I would cross off one square each day until Christmas. And maybe — just maybe — Nannie would come home one of those days.

Snow Day!

I had crossed two days off of my count-down calendar when . . . a snowstorm hit! It came during the night and it woke me up. I could hear the wind howling. I could hear our shutters rattling. So I tiptoed across my room and looked out of the window. Snow was swirling past the light from a street lamp. The ground and street and trees and bushes were covered with white.

"Ooh," I said.

I went back to bed. The next time I woke up it was five o'clock in the morning. Another sound had wakened me. A snowplow was grinding down our street. The *next* time I woke up it was after nine o'clock.

"Nine o'clock!" I cried. I looked outside. Snow, snow everywhere. School must be closed for the day. Mommy had let me sleep late.

I got dressed in a flash and ran downstairs.

"Snow day!" said Mommy.

"Hurray!" I shouted. "Can Nancy and I play outside?"

"Sure," said Mommy. "As soon as you eat breakfast."

I ate quickly. Then I put on snow pants, a sweater, my parka, a scarf, extra socks, my boots, and two pairs of mittens. I walked over to Nancy's. Snow was still falling, but not very hard. A lot had fallen during the night, though.

I was about to climb the steps to Nancy's front porch when the door opened. There was Nancy. She was all dressed up to play in the snow.

64

"*I* was coming over to *your* house!" she said.

Nancy and I flopped onto our backs in the snow. Then we moved our arms and legs up and down, up and down. We stood up carefully.

"Snow angels!" I cried. I drew a halo over my angel's head.

"Let's build Frosty the Snowman," said Nancy. So we did. It was hard work. We rolled and rolled and rolled the snow. The hardest part was putting Frosty's head on his body. The head weighed a ton. But we did it. Then we gave Frosty sticks for arms, a carrot for his nose, stones for his eyes and mouth (we did not have any coal, or even any charcoal briquettes), and a hat and a scarf.

When Frosty was finished, Nancy came to my house for lunch. Then we called Hannie and invited her over to play. The snowplows were clearing the streets, so Mrs. Papadakis said she could drive Hannie over.

All afternoon, Hannie, Nancy, Andrew, and I went sledding down the hill in Nancy's backyard. Sometimes Nancy and I would whiz down the hill together. As we walked back to the top, Nancy would tell me about Hanukkah.

"It's almost the eighth night," she said.

"I know. I can't wait to come over," I replied.

"You know what I got last night?" she said. "Two books."

"Two books?" I repeated in horror. "Which ones?"

"*The Borrowers* and *The Land of Oz*."

Whew! She had not gotten *The Bobbsey Twins in the Mystery Cave*.

"Nancy! Nancy!"

I looked up. Mrs. Dawes was calling Nancy from a window. She called the rest of us, too. "Come on inside for some hot chocolate," she said.

"Oh, boy!" cried Andrew.

We scrambled to the top of the hill. Then

we went into Nancy's house. Mrs. Dawes gave us mugs of hot chocolate with marshmallows floating on top.

I wished that every day could be a snow day.

15

Lighting Candles

It was the eighth night of Hanukkah. Well, actually it was still the afternoon. I was in my room at the little house. I was getting dressed in my party clothes.

"There," I said when I had buckled up my tappy black shoes. "All ready."

I had started to run downstairs when I remembered something. I dashed back to my room and crawled under my bed. I could not forget Nancy's present.

"How do I look?" I asked Mommy when I reached the kitchen.

"Lovely," said Mommy. "Now you better scoot. It's almost sundown." (Nancy had told me to be sure to come to her house before sundown.)

When I rang Nancy's doorbell, I felt a little nervous. I did not know *very* much about Hanukkah. What if I did something wrong tonight?

But I felt better when Mr. Dawes opened the door. "Karen!" he said. "I'm so glad you could join us tonight."

"Thank you," I said.

I stepped inside and took off my coat. Then I carried my present into the living room. There were Nancy, her mother, and Grandma B. (Grandma B is not Nancy's real grandmother. She lives in a nursing home in Stoneybrook. Nancy "adopted" her. Now she is good friends with Nancy *and* Mr. and Mrs. Dawes.)

Everybody said hello. Then Nancy took my hand. She led me to the menorah. The first thing I did was count the candles.

"Hey," I whispered to Nancy. "There are *nine* candles. How come?"

"The extra one is called the *shammash*. It's the helper candle," Nancy explained.

"Oh," I said.

Nancy and her parents and Grandma B and I stood around the menorah. I watched as Mr. Dawes lighted the *shammash* candle. Then he used it to light all the other candles on the menorah. He lighted them from right to left. While he did that, Nancy's family and Grandma B said two prayers. They said them in Hebrew, so I did not understand them, but I liked the way they sounded. The Daweses and Grandma B sang some Hebrew songs, too. After one, Mrs. Dawes said to me, "In English, that's *Rock of Ages*, Karen."

"I know that song!" I exclaimed.

"Mommy, can Karen and I play a dreidel game now?" asked Nancy.

"Of course," said Mrs. Dawes.

"Goody," said Nancy. Then she whispered to me, "Usually I play with Daddy and he always wins!"

Nancy brought out her dreidel and we played the game she had told me about before. Nancy won — three times. But then she said, "Here. I have something for you." She held out her hand. In it was a tiny dreidel. "It's for you. To keep. Now you and Andrew can play at home."

After that, the Daweses and Grandma B gave each other presents. Nancy wasn't kidding. She *did* get a lot of gifts on the last night of Hanukkah. She got Baby Grow-a-Tooth and two more Nintendo games, the skirt, and some other things. Mr. and Mrs. Dawes had also bought *me* two presents — poodle barrettes like Nancy's, and some ribbons for my hair.

"Now," I said, "I have a Hanukkah present for you, Nancy."

Nancy opened the present quickly. For a second she just stared at the book. What was wrong? I wondered. But then Nancy said, "Oh, *thank* you, Karen! This is great!"

I didn't have time to wonder why Nancy had looked so surprised. The Daweses were still opening presents. And then Mr. Dawes gave Nancy and me Hanukkah *gelt* — a little bit of money and some *chocolate* coins! "It's a custom," he said.

After that, we sat down to dinner. I got to taste potato *latkes*. Yum!

And then it was time to go home. Ha-

nukkah was over. I was sad. Now I understood what Hanukkah means to Nancy. I did not feel bad that her family does not celebrate Christmas.

Maybe, I thought, I can celebrate Hanukkah with Nancy again next year.

16

Christmas Eve Day

"*Christmas, Christmas! It's almost here!*" I sang. I was making up my own song. "*Christmas, Christmas! The best time of year!*"

It was early morning on the day before Christmas. I had just woken up. I was lying in bed. I felt warm and snuggly and excited. Friday had been the last day of school. We were on vacation for a week and a half. Later this morning, Andrew and I would go to Daddy's house. There we would see our big-house family . . . except for Nannie.

Suddenly I did not feel excited anymore. Nannie was still in the hospital.

My Christmas wish had not come true.

I had made only *one wish*, and it had *not come true*.

Boo.

I rolled out of bed and got dressed. Then I went downstairs. Maybe I wasn't excited about Christmas, but Andrew was.

"Karen! Karen! It's Christmas Eve!" he cried. "Tonight Santa Claus comes. He'll fill our stockings! Today we go to the big house. Tomorrow we come back here. Two Christmases! Two Christmases!"

Mommy finally had to say, "Settle down, Andrew."

At eleven-thirty in the morning, Andrew and I climbed into our car with Mommy. We were each wearing a backpack. And we were carrying a bag of presents. They were for our big-house family.

"Now remember, Andrew," I said. "The presents are a secret. Don't tell anyone what they are. Nobody is supposed to know until they open them."

"Okay," said Andrew. "Okay, *okay*, OKAY! I love you, Christmas!"

"Settle down, Andrew," said Mommy.

Mommy drove us to the big house. Everyone was waiting for us there. (Everyone except Nannie.) When we walked into the living room I could smell good smells coming from the kitchen. I could hear Christmas

carols playing on the stereo. (*Pa-rum, pum, pum, pum,* went the song about the little drummer boy.) And I saw the big-house Christmas tree. The lights were turned on — tiny bright points of red and blue and gold and green. Andrew's star was on the top of the tree.

Suddenly, I couldn't help feeling Christmasy and excited again, even if my wish had not come true. How could I feel sad? Our tree was sparkly. Emily was getting ready for her first Christmas ever. "Tee?" she said, pointing to the tree. "Pesents?" (There were already some gifts under the tree. They were from friends.)

And everyone seemed to have secrets.

"Don't anyone go in my room," said Kristy. "No peeking today."

"Well, don't anyone go in *my* room," I said as I lugged the bag of presents from Andrew and me up the stairs.

"The attic is off-limits," added Daddy.

After I hid the presents in my closet, I went back downstairs. Everyone was sitting in the living room. They were looking at the tree. David Michael was shaking the presents under it. Charlie was building a fire in the fireplace.

"I hope Santa remembers to come to the big house *and* the little house," said Andrew in a singsong voice.

After awhile, Daddy and Elizabeth stood up. They went into the front hall and put on their coats.

"Where are you going?" I asked.

"Secret mission," said Elizabeth. She was smiling.

Welcome Home, Nannie!

"Secret mission?" I repeated. "What does that mean?"

Kristy shrugged. But I think she knew where Daddy and Elizabeth were going.

After they left, I waited and waited. I stood by the window and watched for Daddy's car. At last I saw it coming down the street.

"They're back!" I shrieked.

I ran to the door. I watched Elizabeth get out of the backseat of the car. Then I watched Daddy get out of the driver's seat and walk around to open the other front door.

Guess who he helped out of the car.

"Nannie!" I cried.

Even though it was freezing cold and snow was on the ground, I raced outside without my coat. I threw my arms around Nannie. "You came back! You're well! You're here in time for Christmas. My wish came true after all!"

I helped Nannie into the house. (She was using a walker.) Everybody wanted to hug Nannie. Finally Elizabeth said, "Okay. Let Nannie sit on the couch. She needs to rest. She's still tired and her hip is a little sore."

Well. Now I *really* felt Christmasy. I began to be excited about opening presents. I hoped it would snow some more. I thought about hanging my stocking and helping Andrew and Emily to leave a snack for Santa. But mostly I was glad Nannie was home. I sat with her all afternoon.

That evening we ate our Christmas dinner — clam chowder first, then turkey and

cranberry dressing and mashed potatoes and apple pie. (I ate everything except the turkey.) After that, my whole big-house family gathered in the living room. First I read *The Night Before Christmas* to everyone. (Andrew always laughs at the "bowlful of jelly" part.) Then Daddy read us the Christmas story from the Bible. I like to imagine Baby Jesus sleeping in the manger of straw. I think that maybe Mary and Joseph and the Wise Men and the shepherds were not the only ones who knew Jesus was special. I think the animals in the stable knew he was special, too.

When Daddy put the Bible away, Elizabeth made hot chocolate. Everyone else (except Nannie) made dashes out of the living room. We returned with presents. Daddy and Elizabeth and Charlie and Sam and Kristy and David Michael brought presents into the living room and put them under the tree. They were presents for Andrew and me. And my brother and I took *our* presents out of the shopping bag and placed them under the tree, too. Only Emily had no gifts to give. Nannie just smiled secretively.

"Can we open the presents now, Daddy?" squealed Andrew.

"Sure," replied Daddy. He put a tape of Christmas carols on the stereo. Then we began to unwrap our packages.

"Goody!" I kept exclaiming. Even though I had not made a list, my family seemed to know what to get me — lots of books. And Daddy bought Baby Grow-a-Tooth!

Even Nannie had presents — leg warmers for me, and a hat for Andrew. She had knitted them while she was in the hospital.

"Oh, boy," said Andrew when the paper and ribbons had been cleared away. "Now it's time to get ready for Santa. I sure hope he comes here tonight. *And* to Mommy's house."

We hung our stockings over the fireplace — ten for us people and one for Boo-Boo and Shannon. Then I showed Emily and Andrew how to leave a snack for Santa.

We gave him milk and cookies. Next to the
snack we left a note. I wrote it for Andrew
and Emily. It said:

DEAR SANTA,
THANK YOU FOR COMING. WE KNOW
YOU ARE VERY BUSY TONIGHT. MERRY
CHRISTMAS! SAY HI TO MRS. CLAUS,
THE ELVES, AND THE REINDEER.
LOVE,
   ANDREW
          AND

EMILY

18

Christmas Day

"Karen! Karen! Wake up! It's Christmas!"

I opened my eyes. My room was very dark. But I could see Andrew standing by my bed. "Merry Christmas," I mumbled.

"Is it six-thirty yet?" asked Andrew.

I looked at my clock. "It's after six-thirty."

"Hurray! We can wake everybody else up then!" (The rule in the big house is that no matter how excited you are on Christmas morning, you can't wake anyone up until six-thirty.)

"Yeah!" I cried. I leapt out of bed.

Andrew and I ran up and down the hallway crying, "It's Christmas! It's Christmas! Wake up!"

Soon Daddy and Elizabeth went downstairs. My brothers and sisters and I sat at the top of the steps and waited to be called. (Nannie was already downstairs. She was sleeping in the den so that she wouldn't have to climb steps.)

"I hear the fire going," said David Michael excitedly.

"I smell coffee," I said.

(When the fire was lit and the coffee was made, Daddy would let us come downstairs and open presents. But not before then.)

"Okay!" Daddy called.

I have never seen seven people rush down the stairs as fast as we did. We dashed for the living room. There was the tree, glowing with lights. There were our stockings. Now they were stuffed. And under the tree was a *huge* pile of presents for my big-house family. I knew none of them were for Andrew and me. We had gotten our presents the night before. I also knew that we would find another pile of presents at Mommy's house later that morning. *Those* presents would be for Andrew and me. (Well, some of them would be.)

"He made it! Santa Claus made it here!" cried Andrew, looking at our stuffed stockings. (The cookies and milk were gone, too.)

We dumped the things out of our stockings in a mad rush. Everyone sat on the floor except for Nannie. She sat on the couch. Inside our stockings were small toys and presents, candy, and a tangerine and some walnuts. Inside Boo-Boo and Shannon's stocking were catnip for Boo-Boo, and chew toys for Shannon. The catnip made Boo-Boo wild. He tore around the house. He pounced on pieces of wrapping paper. He even tried to climb the living-room curtains. Shannon just chewed away happily. But then she discovered that there was candy lying around. She tried to steal it.

Emily looked as if she didn't know *what* was going on.

When our stockings had been emptied, Elizabeth called us into the dining room. We ate breakfast together. Elizabeth had lighted candles and set them on the table. She had put a sprig of holly by each of our places. We ate a Christmas coffee cake and also grapefruit that a friend of Daddy's had sent.

After breakfast, Elizabeth said, "Karen, Andrew. It's time for you to get dressed now. Your mom will be here soon."

So Andrew and I left the table. We changed into party clothes. While we were changing, Daddy and Elizabeth packed up our presents and the things from our stockings. By the time Mommy and Seth arrived we were ready to go. I did not *want* to leave my big-house family, but I was looking forward to another Christmas at the little house.

"Good-bye! Thank you! Merry Christmas!" Andrew and I called as we left.

Seth drove us through Stoneybrook. Andrew and I talked and talked about Christmas. I was gigundo excited.

"Did Santa come to the little house?" asked Andrew anxiously.

"Wait and see," said Mommy.

But what I saw when we reached the little house was Nancy. She was running across our yard. And in her hand she was holding a present. Something about it looked . . . familiar.

Nancy's Present

Seth parked our car. He and Mommy and Andrew and I tumbled out. "Hi, Nancy!" I cried. "Merry Christmas!"

Nancy grinned. "I thought you guys would never get home. I've been watching for you from our front window."

"Well, come on inside," said Seth, as he unlocked the door.

Once again, I walked into a Christmas house. There was our tree with lights and decorations. A pile of presents was under it. And there were the stuffed stockings at the fireplace.

"Santa came here, too!" was the first thing Andrew said.

We hung up our coats and put away our boots. Then Mommy said, "Okay, let's look in our stockings."

"Yea!" I cried. I ran to the mantelpiece. I counted the stockings. One, two, three, four, five, six. "Six!" I exclaimed. "Wait a sec. One for me, one for Andrew, one for Mommy, one for Seth, one for Rocky and Midgie . . ."

"And one for Nancy," Mommy finished.

Nancy *loved* her stocking. "I never had a stocking before," she said.

"And I never had a dreidel until I went to your house for Hanukkah. That's what's fun about trading holidays."

"Yeah," agreed Nancy. "We better do this every year."

Suddenly Andrew cried, "Oh, no! Not again!"

I looked up. Rocky was lying on his back with his feet in the air. He was chewing up a catnip mouse. And Midgie was tunneling under bits of wrapping paper.

Then the doorbell rang. There were Grandma and Grandpa Packett. (They are Mommy's parents. They come for Christmas and Thanksgiving every year.)

"Mommy, can we open our presents now?" asked Andrew as soon as Grandma and Grandpa had taken off their coats.

"Dinner first," said Mommy.

Once again, we sat down to a huge Christmas dinner. (Once again I ate everything except the turkey.)

Then it was time for presents. Andrew and I like to rip into them all at once. But Grandma and Grandpa Packett always say, "Just one present at a time. It's more civilized." (Whatever that means.)

So we took turns opening presents. Mommy and Seth had even bought some gifts for Nancy.

Some of the presents under the tree said

"From Santa" on the tags. Andrew got his Dyno-cars. He and I *each* got the art kit we wanted. And I got more clothes and books and a game called *Sorry!*

"Karen?" said Nancy.

"Yeah?" I was trying on a pair of knee socks with snowflakes on them.

"This is for you." Nancy held out the present she had brought over. The one that looked familiar.

I opened it up. And inside was . . . *The*

Bobbsey Twins in the Mystery Cave! I couldn't believe it.

"Nancy, I — Where did — ?"

"I had already bought it for you when you gave me *my* book," said Nancy. "I found it at an old bookstore. There was only one copy of number fifty-three left."

So *that's* why Nancy had looked so surprised when I had given *her* the book. She'd gotten a copy for me.

Nancy and I smiled at each other. "You know what?" I said. "This must be because we're best friends. Only best friends would give each other the same present."

"Right," agreed Nancy. "And you know what else? This has been the best Hanukkah and the best Christmas ever."

"Definitely," I agreed.

20

Next Year

Late on Christmas afternoon, Grandma and Grandpa Packett went home. Then Nancy went home, too. Mommy and Seth cleaned up the kitchen and the dining room. Andrew and I sat in the living room with our gifts. Andrew crashed his Dyno-cars around. Then he looked inside his art kit. But I opened up my copy of *The Bobbsey Twins* #53. I could not wait to read about Bert and Nan and Freddie and Flossie in a mystery cave.

I read until Mommy said it was time for

supper. I read *during* supper. Then I read after supper while Mommy and Seth put Andrew to bed. By then, I was almost finished with the book. I could have finished it, but I didn't. I wanted to have something to look forward to on the day after Christmas.

Plus, there was something I wanted to do right now, while I was alone in the living room. I put a marker in the book. Then I turned off all the lamps. Only the fire glowed in the fireplace. And the tree lights twinkled in front of the window.

"Good-bye, Christmas," I said softly.

I could not believe that the holidays were almost over. Well, New Year's Eve was just a week away. But New Year's Eve is not my favorite holiday. Christmas is. And it was almost over.

I stared at the tree. I thought about how I had not made a Christmas list because I had had only one wish this year. And suddenly I got one of my ideas. I ran to my room.

In my room I found a piece of paper and a crayon. I began to make a list.

My list was just finished when Mommy came in. "Karen," she said, "it's bedtime." She peered at my paper. "What are you doing?"

"I'm making a Christmas list," I told her. "I never gave you one."

"But, honey," Mommy said. (She sounded confused.) "Christmas is over."

"I know," I replied. "This is what I want *next* year."

Mommy took the list. She read it.

Here is what I had written down:

I WANT:
1. MY TWO FAMILIES TO BE HEALTHY. (NO ONE IN THE HOSPITAL.)
2. EVERYONE IN MY TWO FAMILIES TO BE HOME FOR CHRISTMAS.
3. TO CELEBRATE HANUKKAH WITH NANCY.
4. NANCY TO CELEBRATE CHRISTMAS WITH US.
5. NO MORE PLANE CRASHES.
6. NO MORE BOMBS OR WARS.

7. HOUSES FOR EVERYBODY IN THE WORLD TO LIVE IN.
8. NO GUNS.
9. RICKY TORRES TO ASK ME TO MARRY HIM.
10. THREE MADAME ALEXANDER DOLLS.

Mommy finished reading the list. She smiled at me.

"I'm just getting a head start," I told her.

"Okay. I'll save the list for next year," said Mommy. "Now it's time for you to get into your nightgown."

So I did. I climbed into bed with Goosie and Tickly.

"Merry Christmas, sweetie," said Mommy.

Seth poked his head into my room. "Merry Christmas, Karen!"

"Good night and Merry Christmas," I replied.

Holiday Activities for You to Try

These are some of Karen's favorites—so you can be sure they're gigundo fun!

Countdown to Christmas Calendar!

When the calendar turns to December, grown-ups like to say that Christmas is just around the corner. But to Karen, December 25 seems a long way off, so sometimes she makes this Countdown to Christmas Advent calendar. It makes the time go faster.

You will need:
1 large sheet red construction paper
1 large sheet green construction paper
glue
scissors
crayons

Here's what you do:
1. Cut a large Christmas tree out of the green paper.
2. Cut 24 little doors into the tree. Make sure the doors open and close.
3. Glue your tree to the red paper.
4. Decorate the inside of each door. Use your crayons to draw pictures of tree ornaments, presents, Santa, or anything that reminds you of Christmas.

5. Close all the doors. Number all the doors as you see in the picture.

6. Each day, beginning at the top of the tree, open the door that shows what day of the month it is. When you reach the last door . . . `hooray! It's Christmas Eve!

Clay Menorah

Each night of Hanukkah, Nancy and her family light the menorah. You can make your very own menorah. Here's how.

You will need:
1 cup flour
½ cup salt
⅓ cup water
food coloring
1 Hanukkah candle

Here's what you do:
1. Mix the flour and salt together in a bowl.
2. Pour the water in, a little bit at a time, kneading the clay until it is smooth.
3. To color the clay, work a few drops of food coloring into it as you knead.
4. Form your clay into any shape you like. (A menorah doesn't have to look like a nine-branched candleholder.) Just make sure your menorah is at least ½-inch thick in any place where you want to put the candles.

5. Use the bottom of your candle to make nine holes in the clay. The holes should be about ½-inch deep, in order to hold the candle. Be careful not to poke the candle all the way through the clay.

6. Let your menorah dry overnight.

Happy candlelight!

An A-door-able Holiday Wreath!

You will need:
1 paper plate
glue
green tissue paper
red crepe paper

Here's what you do:
1. Cut out the center of the paper plate so only the outer circle is left.
2. Cut the tissue paper into many 2-by-2-inch squares.
3. Roll one of the squares into a cone-shaped tissue-paper bud.
4. Dab some glue onto the bottom end of the bud.
5. Glue your tissue-paper bud to the wreath.
6. Keep adding more buds to the wreath until the whole circle is covered with tissue-paper buds.
7. Make a bow from the red crepe paper.
8. Glue the bow to the bottom of your wreath.

The Very First Christmas Tree

Nancy trimmed *her* first Christmas tree at Karen's house. But she wanted to know about the *real* first Christmas tree. There are lots of stories about why people bring trees into their houses and decorate them. Karen told Nancy her favorite story. Here's what she said:

"The first Christmas tree was a poor little fir tree in the stable where Jesus was born. It watched all the shepherds and the Three Wise Men bring gifts to Jesus. The tree felt sad that it didn't have a gift. God saw how bad the tree felt, so He told the stars in the sky to go to the tree. When they did, they rested on the tree's branches and made the tree beautiful. The tree felt happy. It looked pretty for Jesus. Ever since, people have decorated trees. First they decorated them with candles. Now they decorate them with lights and ornaments."

There are other stories about Christmas trees. Some people say that the decorations symbolize

the gifts the Wise Men brought to Jesus. Others like the story about a man named Martin Luther, who found a fir tree in the woods and decided to bring it home to his children. It looked beautiful when starlight shone on it through a window.

But Karen's favorite story is the one she told Nancy!

Tree Trimmers!

These easy-to-make ornaments are real treats for your tree!

Tiny Boxes

You will need:
small gift boxes (like the kind jewelry comes in)
wrapping paper
tape or glue
brightly colored yarn
small paper clips

Here's what you do:
1. Wrap each box in wrapping paper.
2. Use tape or glue to hold the paper together.
3. Tie each of the boxes with a bow of brightly colored yarn.
4. Use a paper clip as a hook.
5. Hang your gift boxes from the tree.

Fun Felt Ornaments

You will need:
1 sheet of thin cardboard (the kind your dad's shirts are packed in)
2 pieces of felt
Magic Markers
glue
scissors
cotton balls
glitter
yarn

Here's what you do:
1. Decide what shape you want your ornament to be. Draw that shape on the cardboard.
2. Cut out the shape.
3. Place the cardboard shape on one piece of felt. Trace around the shape with the Magic Marker. Cut out the shape. Repeat the same step on the second piece of felt.
4. Glue one piece of cut felt to the front of the cardboard shape. Glue the second piece of cut felt to the back of the cardboard shape.

5. Decorate your ornament any way you like. If you decide to decorate your ornament with glitter, first spread a thin layer of glue where you want the glitter to go. Then sprinkle glitter on the ornament. The glitter will stick only where there is glue.

6. Glue a loop of yarn to the top of the back of your ornament. Use the loop to hang your felt ornament on your tree for everyone to see.

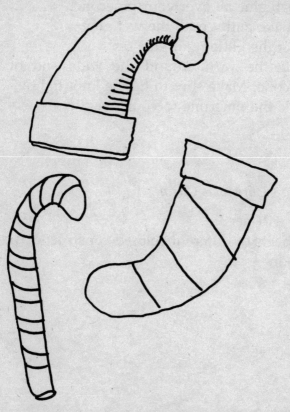

Fine Pinecone Ornament

You will need:
1 medium-sized pinecone
glue
glitter
yarn

Here's what you do:
1. Dab glue all over your pinecone.
2. Shake glitter onto the wet glue.
3. Let the glitter and glue dry.
4. Tie the yarn around the wide end of your pinecone. Make sure to tie the knot tightly.
5. Tie the pinecone to your tree.

Karen's Christmas Chain

You will need:
12 sheets of different-colored construction paper
scissors
glue

114

Here's what you do:

1. Cut the paper into strips. Each strip should be about one inch wide and six inches long.

2. Roll the first strip into a circle.

3. Glue the ends together.

4. Put one end of the next strip through the circle.

5. Glue the ends of the second strip together to form a circle.

6. Keep going until you have a long chain to swirl around your tree.

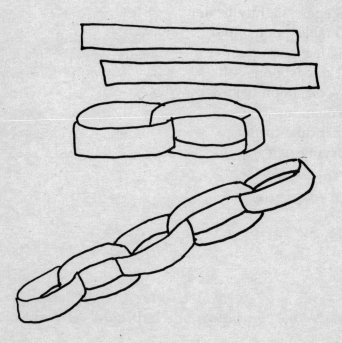

Luscious Latkes

Mrs. Dawes made Hanukkah latkes for Nancy and Karen. Karen thought they were yummy! Here's a recipe for potato latkes. You can help with the mixing. But when it comes to the frying, let a grown-up do the work.

You will need:
9 medium-sized potatoes
3 small onions, chopped
salad oil
3 eggs, slightly beaten
3 tablespoons flour
¼ teaspoon pepper
1½ teaspoons salt
¾ teaspoon baking powder
collander
pancake turner
frying pan

116

Here's what you do:

1. Wash the potatoes thoroughly.
2. Grate the potatoes.
3. Let the grated potatoes sit for 10 minutes. Then, using a collander, get rid of any excess water.
4. Fry the chopped onions in just enough salad oil to cover the bottom of the frying pan.
5. Add the fried onions to the drained potatoes. Stir in the eggs.
6. Add the flour, pepper, salt, and baking powder. Mix thoroughly.
7. Drop the batter by tablespoons into a large frying pan with about ¼ inch of hot salad oil. Flatten with a metal pancake turner.
8. When the latkes become brown, turn and brown on the other side.
9. Drain cooked latkes on paper towels.
10. Serve with applesauce or sour cream.
Mmm! They're gigundo good!

What a Card!

These holiday cards have a fun twist to them!

Jigsaw Jolly Holiday Card

You will need:
construction paper
crayons
scissors
1 envelope

Here's what you do:
1. Draw a holiday picture on construction paper.
2. Write a message on the back of your picture and sign your name.
3. Cut your picture into pieces, like the ones in a jigsaw puzzle.
4. Put all the pieces in the envelope.
5. Write this message on the envelope: *Put me together to find a secret holiday message!*
6. Give the card to someone who makes you fall to pieces.

A Shimmering Snow Card

You will need:
salt
crayons
tempera paints
paintbrushes
construction paper

Here's what you do:
1. Fold the paper like a card.
2. Write a message on the inside of your card.
3. Paint a snowy scene on the front of your card.
4. While the paint is still wet, sprinkle salt wherever you want your picture to shimmer and shine.
5. Let the paint dry. Then give the card to your favorite shining star.

Great Gift Ideas

Everyone will love these perfect presents. You can make them with things you find around the house!

I'll Do It for You IOU

Does you dad hate doing the dishes? Is your mother tired of making the beds? Is your sister tired of taking out the trash? Then how about giving them the perfect gift—a day off from their chores?

GIFT CERTIFICATE

THIS CERTIFICATE ENTITLES

_____
NAME

TO HAVE _____
NAME

DO _____
FILL IN CHORE

FOR _____
AMOUNT OF TIME

SIGNED _____
YOUR NAME

You will need:
construction paper
crayons
gift box
bow

Here's what you do:
1. Copy the IOU certificate on page 121.
2. Write in your name, the name of the person you are giving the certificate to, the type of chore you are going to do, and how long you will do it for. Here are some ideas for your certificates.
  - do the dishes
  - make the beds
  - set the table
  - take out the garbage
  - play quiet games with your little brother or sister
  - fold the laundry
  - rake the leaves
  - help shovel snow
3. Put the certificate in the gift box and finish it off with a pretty holiday bow.

Everyone in Ms. Colman's second-grade class knows how to make these necklace and pencil cup presents. They made them for their friends at Stoneybrook Manor for Grandparents' Day.

Very Merry Macaroni Necklaces

You will need:
macaroni (all shapes and sizes)
yarn
tempera paint
paintbrushes

Here's what you do:
1. Paint the macaroni any way you want. (Karen likes polka dots!) Make sure the macaroni is dry, not cooked. Cooked macaroni would be too slimy! Wait until the paint is dry, too.
2. String the macaroni onto a long piece of yarn.
3. Tie the ends of the yarn into a knot.
Wow! What a pretty necklace!

Orange-You-Glad Pencil Cups

You will need:
1 frozen orange juice or soup can (make sure it is clean and dry)
holiday wrapping paper
glue
scissors

Here's what you do:
1. Cut a sheet of wrapping paper. Make sure you cut it so that the paper is as tall as the can and long enough to wrap all the way around it.
2. Spread glue on the back of the wrapping paper.
3. Wrap the paper around the can so that the glue sticks to it.

That's the *write* way to make this pencil cup!

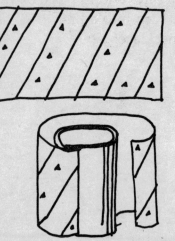
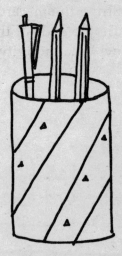

That's a Wrap!

Everyone will notice your present when it's wrapped up like a snowman.

You will need:
1 rectangular box
white wrapping paper
cotton balls
black paint
scissors
glue
2 cardboard tubes from paper-towel rolls
orange construction paper
crepe paper

Here's what you do:
1. Put your gift in the box.
2. Cover the box with white paper.
3. Dip cotton balls in black paint.
4. To make the eyes, mouth, and buttons, glue the black cotton balls onto the box as you see in the picture on page 125.
5. Make an orange construction-paper cone. Glue the cone where the snowman's nose should be.
6. Cover the cardboard tubes with white paper. Glue them onto the box as you see in the picture.
7. Make a red crepe-paper bow. Tie it around the snowman's neck.

Super Spinning Dreidel

Nancy gave Karen a dreidel. Now you can have one, too!

You will need:
1 egg carton
1 small pencil
scissors

Here's what you do:

1. Cut one egg section from the carton.
2. Have a grown-up poke a hole right through the center of the egg section.
3. Draw the Hebrew letters

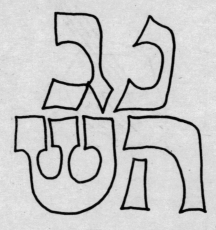

on the four sides of the egg section.
4. Poke the pencil through the hole.
5. Look in Chapter 12 to see how Nancy told Karen how to play dreidel.

Hope you win the game!

Holidays Around the World!

In December, people all over the world celebrate Christmas and Hanukkah. Not everyone celebrates holidays as we do in America.

• In France and Spain, children put shoes by the fireplace and wait for Santa Claus to fill them with sweets and small toys.

• Chinese children decorate their homes with paper lanterns for Christmas. They call Santa *Dun Che Lao*.

• In December, the weather in Australia is warm and sunny. On Christmas day, Australian families have big picnics on the beach.

• Mexican children play the piñata game on Christmas day. A piñata is an animal made of papier-mâché. In the game, a piñata is filled with candy and toys. Children take turns putting on a blindfold and trying to break the piñata with a stick. Everyone gets a turn until the piñata is broken. Then there is a mad scramble to pick up the candy and toys!

• In Israel, children eat sweet jelly-filled donuts on Hanukkah. The donuts are called *soofganiyot*.

• All over the world, the letters on a dreidel mean "a great miracle happened there." *There* means *Israel*. So in Israel, the last letter on a dreidel is different. The letters on Israeli dreidels stand for "a great miracle happened *here*."

Sweet-as-Sugar Sugar Cookies

Christmastime means cookie time! Karen loves her mom's holiday sugar cookies. This is how Mrs. Engle makes them. Ask your mom or dad to help you make cookies, too!

You will need:
1 cup butter
⅔ cup sugar
1 egg
1 teaspoon vanilla extract
2½ cups sifted flour
½ teaspoon salt
rolling pin
2 mixing bowls: 1 large, 1 smaller
cookie sheet

Here's what you do:
1. Mix the butter and the sugar together.
2. Beat in the egg and vanilla.
3. In a separate mixing bowl, combine the flour and salt.
4. Add the egg mixture to the flour mixture, and stir.
5. Chill the dough for three hours.
6. Preheat your oven to 350 degrees F.
7. On a flour-covered, clean, flat surface, roll out the dough to ⅛-inch thickness.

8. Use cookie cutters to cut your cookies into holiday shapes.

9. Bake cookies on a greased cookie sheet for about eight minutes.

The Story of Befana

Christmas is a time for telling Christmas stories. Karen and Andrew especially like this tale about a woman named Befana.

Befana was very old and cranky. She lived in Italy a long time ago — around the time Jesus was born. Befana wasn't kind to anyone. She would not ask tired travelers to rest in her home. She would not even give them a hot meal before they continued on their journey. Befana cared about only one thing — cleaning her house. She cleaned day and night, which is why she was always so cranky.

One night three wise men came to Befana's door. They told the old woman that they were headed for Bethlehem to greet the Baby Jesus. They had special gifts for Him. But the Wise Men were lost. They needed Befana to travel with them. They needed her to guide them to Bethlehem.

As usual, Befana refused to help. She angrily told the Wise Men that she would not leave her nice, warm house to travel all the way to Bethlehem. Then she asked them to leave right away!

The next morning, Befana felt bad about the Wise Men. She remembered their kind faces, and how much they wanted to give gifts to Jesus. She decided she wanted to help the Wise Men. Befana put on her shoes and shawl. She gathered up some gifts for the Baby Jesus. Then she ran out after the Three Wise Men. But she could not find them. And to this day, Befana roams the earth, carrying gifts and searching for the Wise Men. And every year, on Christmas Eve, her gifts go to good boys and girls all over the world.

Holiday Puzzles!

Hooray! The holidays are here! Holiday puzzles bring good cheer!

Hanukkah's Here!

Hanukkah starts tonight. It's time to take out the menorah. Help Nancy and her mother find their menorah. Color in all the spaces that equal eight.

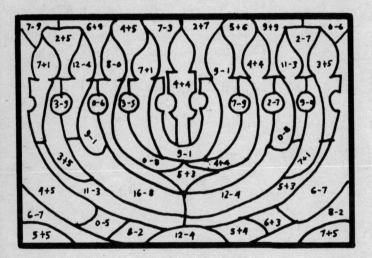

Reindeer Wordsearch

Help Hannie find the names of Santa's reindeer in this wordsearch. The names go up, down, sideways, backwards, and diagonally.

Look for: Cupid, Dasher, Dancer, Prancer, Vixen, Rudolph, Blitzen, Comet, and Donder.

```
H  D  I  P  U  C  R  V  N
O  A  K  N  C  D  E  I  E
K  S  P  O  L  A  D  X  Z
C  H  M  N  B  S  N  E  T
E  E  C  A  D  B  O  N  I
T  R  E  C  N  A  D  V  L
P  R  A  N  C  E  R  H  B
A  S  H  P  L  O  D  U  R
```

Here Comes Santa Claus Maze

Help Santa deliver presents to the big house, the little house, Hannie's house, and Ricky's house. Solve the maze.

What's in the Box Dot-to-Dot

Kristy doesn't want anyone to peek at her presents! Karen is dying to know what's in her box. To find out what's in the box, count by twos to connect the dots.

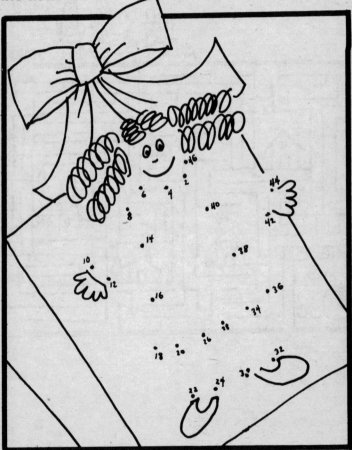

About the Author

ANN M. MARTIN lives in New York City and loves animals. Her cat, Mouse, knows how to take the phone off the hook.

Other books by Ann M. Martin that you might enjoy are *Stage Fright, Me and Katie (the Pest)*, and the books in *The Baby-sitters Club* series.

Ann likes ice cream, the beach, and *I Love Lucy*. And she has her own little sister, whose name is Jane.

MAKE A WISH...
AND SEE IF IT COMES TRUE!

Enter the

BABY·SITTERS

Little Sister™

Make-a-Wish Giveaway!

Do you have one special holiday wish? Roller skates? A bike? Let us know! Win and we'll grant you your wish (valued up to $100). Just fill in the coupon below and return it by March 31, 1991.

Rules: Entries must be postmarked by March 31, 1991. Winners will be picked at random and notified by mail. No purchase necessary. Void where prohibited. Taxes on prizes are the responsibility of the winners and their immediate families. Employees of Scholastic Inc.; its agencies, affiliates, subsidiaries; and their immediate families not eligible. For a complete list of winners, send a self-addressed stamped envelope to: Baby-sitters Little Sister Make-a-Wish Giveaway, Winners List, at the address provided below.

Fill in the coupon below or write the information on a 3" x 5" piece of paper and mail to: **BABY-SITTERS LITTLE SISTER MAKE-A-WISH GIVEAWAY,** P.O. Box 753, 730 Broadway, New York, NY 10003. Canadian residents send entries to: Iris Ferguson, Scholastic Inc., 123 Newkirk Road, Richmond Hill, Ontrario, Canada L4C365.

Baby-sitters Little Sister Make-a-Wish Giveaway

My special holiday wish is _____

_____

Name _____ Age _____

Street _____

City_____ State _____ Zip _____

Where did you buy this *Baby-sitters Little Sister* book?

☐ Bookstore   ☐ Drugstore   ☐ Supermarket   ☐ Library
☐ Book Club   ☐ Book Fair   ☐ Other_____(specify)

BLS690